First published in Great Britain in 1990 by The Bodley Head Children's Books

This edition published in Great Britain in 2007 and in the USA in 2008 by
Frances Lincoln Children's Books, 4 Torriano Mews,
Torriano Avenue, London NW5 2RZ
www.franceslincoln.com

British Library Cataloguing in Publication Data available on request

ISBN 978-1-84507-720-4

Printed in Singapore

9 8 7 6 5 4 3 2 1

GOING TO PLAYSCHOOL

Sarah Garland

F
FRANCES LINCOLN
CHILDREN'S BOOKS

We're off to playschool.

Here we are,

and here's your peg.

Time for a game,

then pouring sand,

rolling out pastry,

painting pictures,

dressing up and

undressing.

A rest and a drink of juice,

then outside to play.

Look at the rabbit!

Say hello! In he goes!

Here's your friend!

A story before we go home.

Coats on, boots on,

but where's Blue Rabbit?

Here he is! He likes playschool!